W9-BSD-088

NO FAIR! NO FAIR!

And Other Jolly Poems of Childhood

Poems by Calvin Trillin * Pictures by Roz Chast

Orchard Books   New York   An Imprint of Scholastic Inc.

Text copyright © 2016 by Calvin Trillin
Illustrations copyright © 2016 by Roz Chast

All rights reserved. Published by Orchard Books, an imprint of Scholastic Inc., *Publishers since 1920.*
ORCHARD BOOKS and design are registered trademarks of Watts Publishing Group, Ltd., used under license.
SCHOLASTIC and associated logos are trademarks and/or registered trademarks of Scholastic Inc.

The publisher does not have any control over and does not assume any responsibility for author or
third-party websites or their content.

No part of this publication may be reproduced, stored in a retrieval system, or transmitted in any
form or by any means, electronic, mechanical, photocopying, recording, or otherwise, without written
permission of the publisher. For information regarding permission, write to Scholastic Inc.,
Attention: Permissions Department, 557 Broadway, New York, NY 10012.

This book is a work of fiction. Names, characters, places, and incidents are either the product of the
author's imagination or are used fictitiously, and any resemblance to actual persons, living or dead,
business establishments, events, or locales is entirely coincidental.

Library of Congress Cataloging-in-Publication Data
Trillin, Calvin.
[Poems. Selections]
No fair! No fair!: and other jolly poems of childhood / by Calvin Trillin ; illustrated by Roz Chast.
pages ; cm   ISBN 978-0-545-82578-8
I. Chast, Roz, illustrator. II. Title.
PS3570.R5A6 2016   811.54—dc23   2015031338

10 9 8 7 6 5 4 3 2 1   16 17 18 19 20
Printed in China 62

Book design by Charles Kreloff and David Saylor
The artwork was created with ink and watercolor.
First edition, October 2016

To Isabelle and Toby and Rebecca
and Natey, of course
– CT

COULD JENNY GET THIS SHOT FOR ME?
I'VE DONE SO MUCH FOR HER!

I know this shot will guard me from the measles and the mumps —
Diseases that could leave me with two different kinds of lumps.
I'm glad the stuff that's in the shot will keep me safe from harm,
But can't they put the needle into someone else's arm?
If so, my older sister is the person I'd prefer.
Could Jenny get this shot for me? I've done so much for her.

You once read her a fairy tale she loved, and ever since
She's thought a certain frog, if kissed, would turn into a prince.
Remember what I did for her? I'm sure you didn't miss it.
I threw my pet frog in her lap, and then I said, "So, kiss it."
That frog was only one of many favors that there were.
Could Jenny get this shot for me? I've done so much for her.

Once, Jenny, on a summer day, was in her party clothes,
And, seeing just how hot she was, I sprayed her with the hose.
Once, noticing how much the same her dollies all appeared,
I gave one doll a different look by drawing on a beard.
She has to be so grateful for my favors — there've been many.
So could she get this shot for me? I've done so much for Jenny.

EATING HABITS

Matt loved the food most kids considered weird.
Weird food from this boy's plate just disappeared.
He loved stuff that had French names or Italian.
He'd chew up raw a scallop or a scallion.
He gnawed on wings of pigeons and of quails.
He loved both bull-foot soup and gator tails.
He'd eat the sort of insides that you might
Prefer to keep inside and out of sight.
At times, he'd have for lunch some fried croquettes
Of things that other people keep for pets.
(He once had eaten turtle in a stew —
Though not, it's true, a turtle that he knew.)
His tum, it seemed at times, was nearly bottomless.
His dad said, "Matt would eat a hippopotamus."

The neighbors were amazed. They'd never seen
A sight like this — a boy who seemed so keen
On eating what could make a strong man cower.
They gathered round to see what he'd devour.
Dad beamed as Matt ate liver from a duck.
Matt's little sister shivered, and said, "Yuck!"

JOHN HENRY, NINA, AND THE BLUE HYENA

Hyenas, unlike mute giraffes,
Make noises sounding much like laughs.
This town had in its lovely zoo
A large hyena that was blue.
It was, because of that strange shade,
The rarest of the beasts displayed.
Two kids, while standing just outside
Its cage thought they would like a ride —
On top, just like a luggage rack,
Atop that blue hyena's back.
They said to the hyena, "Please."
He smiled, and jumped the fence with ease.

John Henry and his sister, Nina,
Then climbed aboard this blue hyena,
Who said, "Now kindly get strapped in.
Where should this spin of ours begin?"
"The shopping mall, of course," said John.
So, like a smoothly swimming swan,
The blue hyena took them there,
Then to a park, then to a fair,
Then quickly past a vast arena —
All still atop that blue hyena.

They heard this shouted by a cop:
"Hey, look! What's that he's got on top?
Why, this is new! I've never seen a
Delivery by blue hyena."
They passed some bikes; they passed some cars.
They waved. They felt like movie stars,
Or like a famous ballerina
Out riding on her blue hyena.

Then, in this outing's final stage,
The beast jumped back into his cage,
And landed with a mighty whack.
But first the kids climbed off his back.
And then John Henry's sister, Nina,
Said this to thank the blue hyena:
"You're special being blue in color.
(The other colors are much duller.)
More special, though, than even that,
We thought as on your back we sat,
Of all the beasts that we have tried,
You really give the smoothest ride.
Another way that you're unique:
Hyenas laugh, but most don't speak."

HOW MANY STUFFED ANIMALS?

Stuffed animals sleep in a pile in my bed.
How many do you think there might be?
How many stuffed animals piled in my bed
Would still leave enough room for me?

Just guess at the number of animal pals
I have as I drift off to sleep.
Yes, figure out how many teddies and such
Are piled upon me in a heap.

A hint: that big dog I was given last year,
The one with red eyes and blue hair,
Made twenty-two dogs that I had in my bed
(Though some people think he's a bear).

Give up? You can't guess what the answer could be?
Okay, here it is: I've got eighty
Stuffed-animal pals who all sleep in my bed.
My mom thinks the pile's getting weighty.

She knows that at night, when I turn in my sleep,
Some pals may get knocked to the floor.
So Mom said that I should get rid of a few.
And I said, "I really need more."

For instance, I do have six moose and a pig.
I've got three white lambs plus their mother.
But one tiny panda is all that I've got.
One panda! I should have another.

The animal pals that are piled in my bed
Keep nighttime from being much scarier.
That's why I need more. I've got plenty of room.
For me, it's the more pals the merrier.

LEARNING TO TIE YOUR SHOES

My friend Jerome can't tie his shoes himself.
"So you should learn," I often tell Jerome.
"You should know how to tie your shoes, in case
You ever want to run away from home."

You have to learn to tie your shoes yourself
If you're to run away to far-off places.
'Cause otherwise, before you got too far,
You might be tripping over dangling laces.

NO.

NOPE.

NO SIRREE, BOB.

YES!

WHO PLAYS WHAT

I like all our games of pretending,
But why is it always routine
That I am the queen's loyal servant
And Claudia's always the queen?

At times we are both busy building
A passenger spaceship with chairs.
Then she is the astronaut captain.
And me? I'm collecting the fares.

She always decides what the game is.
It's true that she's older, of course.
But why is she always the sheriff
While I'm always playing her horse?

WHO'S THE AWFULEST KID IN YOUR CLASS?

"Who's the awfulest kid in your class?"
My uncle Joe asks when we meet.
"Who's the meanest of boys?
Who will not share his toys?
Who at games is most likely to cheat?"

"Who's the terriblest kid in the group?"
My uncle Joe's eager to know.
"Who annoys you a bunch?
Who might well steal your lunch?
While he shoves you or steps on your toe?"

Though no kid in my class is that bad,
Joe needed some sort of reply.
So, then, here's what I did:
I invented a kid
Who's a bully — a really mean guy.

So whenever I see Uncle Joe,
I tell him that Justin's still naughty:
"He still shouts and he'll swear.
He will bite and pull hair.
Justin oughtn't to do such things, ought he!"

I say Justin is still in my class,
And for awfulness no one can beat him.
Justin strikes Uncle Joe
As a guy he should know.
I just hope Joe won't ask now to meet him.

THE GRANDPA RULE IS IN EFFECT

Whenever Grandpa's minding us,
There's just one rule we must respect:
To do what we would like to do.
The Grandpa Rule is in effect.

No time we have to be in bed?
That sort of thing's what we expect
When Grandpa is the one in charge.
The Grandpa Rule is in effect.

"To spoil you is my job," he says.
"A job that I will not neglect.
All rules are off, except for one:
The Grandpa Rule is in effect."

Our mom pretends she doesn't know —
Not even if the house seems wrecked
When she returns. But she must know
The Grandpa Rule was in effect.

THE BACKSEAT

The backseat is a space we always share,
Which should mean half and half — that's only fair.
Imagine, then, a line right down the middle —
A line with which we've promised not to fiddle.
It's meant to keep us each in our own section.
But wait! She's scooching now in my direction.

She's over the line,
She's over the line.
She occupies space
That's rightfully mine.

She's looking out my window once again.
Although it's mine, she'll sneak a look, and then
She'll slowly, slowly, slowly start to slide
Till parts of her are clearly on my side.
"Get back! Get back!" I constantly repeat.
"You really don't need more than half a seat."

She's over the line,
She's over the line.
She's camping out now
On space that is mine.

She knows that what she's doing is improper.
But on she comes, and how am I to stop her?
'Cause even if that scooch becomes a skitter,
My dad says that I'm not allowed to hit her.
There's just one way to stop her sneaky tricks:
I'll build a wall along the line — with bricks.

FOUR MORNING COMPLAINTS

GETTING DRESSED
Oh, this is such a silly rule —
That people must wear pants to school.
A better rule, a wise man said,
Is wear your underpants instead.

EATING BREAKFAST
I know this oatmeal's very good
For little boys, except I would
Prefer some ice cream, if it's handy —
With cookie bits and chocolate candy.

GOING TO SCHOOL
The bus is slow, without a doubt.
And all the kids get tossed about.
Let's scrap the bus. That's my advice.
A helicopter might be nice.

SHARING A SCHOOL BUS SEAT
Jack's body's big, and then it spreads.
His elbows poke. His jacket sheds.
A guy as big as Jack has grown
Should have a bus that's all his own.

TO GET A PET

I kept on asking for a pet
For me and for my sister, Bette.
We hoped a dog was what we'd get —
The furriest you'd ever met.
Our parents said, in Russian, "Nyet.
You're both too young, so no pet yet."
So we said, "You would not regret
This pet. Its care would be all set —
All done by us without a sweat
(Except for driving to the vet)."
At last, Mom said, "You'd like, I'll bet,
A goldfish, reachable by net."
"A fish!" we said. "But fish are wet.
We want a pet that we can pet!"

We finally got a furry puppy,
He's soft, and drier than a guppy.

STUDYING THE BUTTERFLY
Though butterflies are cool, all right,
Instead of them I thought we might
Put action figures on the floor
And fight a superhero war.

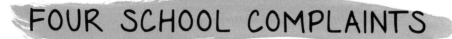

BEING BOSSED
Vanessa's bossy as can be.
The one she loves to boss is me.
I really wish that she had found
Another kid to boss around.

BEING CHOSEN
I'm chosen first when we choose teams,
But that is only in my dreams.
I still don't know what it might take
To be the first when I'm awake.

BEING CALLED ON
Because she likes to use real names,
My teacher always calls me James.
But nicknames are the names I like.
I really wish she'd call me Spike.

BABY BROTHER BILLY

Our baby brother finally came.
We call him Billy. That's his name.
He isn't old enough to play.
He only cries and poops all day.
He cannot throw. He cannot run.
This baby brother's not much fun.
I said to my big brother, Zach,
"So maybe we should send him back."

Our mom then said, "You're being silly.
We certainly are keeping Billy.
We all have jobs. Mine's in a shop,
And, as you know, your dad's a cop.
You have a job — a job that's cool.
Your job is that you go to school.
Now Billy's newly joined our group.
It's Billy's job to cry and poop."

EVENING COMPLAINTS

NOT WATCHING CARTOONS
In school we're studying baboons.
Baboons are featured in cartoons.
So if cartoons are just like school,
Why have this anticartoon rule?
An ape's an ape, no matter where.
No fair, no fair, no fair, no fair.

DOING HOMEWORK
Math homework now? It seems to me
I ought to play or watch TV.
There's no way I could learn much more.
I know that two and two are four.
I know a circle from a square.
No fair, no fair, no fair, no fair.

TAKING A BATH
You said that it is not all right
For me to skip a bath tonight.
I have to take one, even though
I took a bath two days ago.
You even said, "Let's wash that hair."
No fair, no fair, no fair, no fair.

GOING TO BED
Though Nate stays up, to me you've said,
"Okay, my friend, it's time for bed."
I'll bet when I'm as old as Nate,
You still won't let me stay up late.
I'll say, "I'm eight," but you won't care.
No fair, no fair, no fair, no fair.

AUTHOR'S NOTE

Once, when I was visiting my daughter Sarah and her family, my younger grandson, Natey, who was then about six, was slow about getting dressed for school.

"Please put your pants on, Natey," Sarah said.

Without giving the matter much thought, I found that I had a song to sing about that:

> "Oh, this is such a silly rule —
> That people must wear pants to school.
> A better rule, a wise man said,
> Is wear your underpants instead."

That is still the song Natey and I sing when we feel the need to perform a duet. (When I sing with Natey's older brother, Toby, we tend to go with a Glasgow street song entitled "Oh, You Cannae Shove Your Granny Off a Bus.")

A lot of the poems in this book were inspired by real-life experience — although not as directly as the poem about Natey's pants. For instance, one of my nephews, when arriving at the doctor's office for a scheduled shot, really did ask his mother if she could take the shot for him. ("I'll just wait here in the car.") A grandchild of mine does share a bed — a rather small bed — with several dozen stuffed animals. Our family still observes the Grandpa Rule, under which the only rule when Grandpa is in charge is that there are no rules. My daughters, we learned after they were grown, used to play a game in which my older daughter was always the queen and her younger sister was always the slave. "We want a pet we can pet" was chanted by my granddaughters, Isabelle and Rebecca, and their friends Olivia and Nora. I did indeed spend what seemed like a good part of my childhood protecting my half of the backseat from the scooching tactics of my slightly older sister, Sukey the Oppressor.

I thank everybody involved for the inspiration — even Sukey.

— Calvin Trillin